Min Monkey Little and Lemur

by Jay Dale

"Look, Grandpa Tut!"
said Min Monkey.
"I can see a ladybird.
It can go **UP** and **down**."

Flit!

2

Flit! Flit!

"Can I look, too?" said Little Lemur.

"You can look, too!" said Min Monkey.

"Oh!" said Little Lemur.

"The ladybird is on this orange flower."

"Here is a little green frog," said Min Monkey.

"It can go **up** and **down**."

Hop!

"The little green frog can go in the big blue pond," said Little Lemur.

Hop!

Hop!

"I can go in the big blue pond, too!"

said Min Monkey.

"Look at me! Look at me!

I can go **up** and **down**."

Splash!

Splash! Splash!

"I can go in the big blue pond, too!"
said Little Lemur.

"I can go **up** and **down!**
Look at me!"

Splish!

Splish!

Splish!

"Oh, no," said Little Lemur.

"I can see a big green crocodile!"

Eeeeek!

"Eeeeek!" said Min Monkey.

"I can see it, too!"

"I can go up this big tree,"
said Little Lemur.

"I can go **up**, **up**, **up** ...

1, 2, 3!"

"I can, too," said Min Monkey.
"I can go **up**, **up**, **up** ...
1, 2, 3!"

Zip!

Zip!

"Look!" said Little Lemur.

"I can see a butterfly on this green leaf."

"I can see it, too," said Min Monkey.

"The butterfly is red and blue."

"Oh, no," said Little Lemur.

"I can see a big brown snake!"

"Eeeek!" said Min Monkey.

"I can see it, too!"

"I can go down this big tree,"
said Little Lemur.

"I can go

down, down, down ...

3, 2, 1!"

"I can go down this big tree, too."

said Min Monkey.

"I can go **down, down, down** ...
3, 2, 1!"

"I can run!" said Little Lemur.

"I can run, too!" said Min Monkey.

Yippee!

Yippee!